I0843509

Miracle Of the Shattered Blade

ALICIA MORTON

WORKBOOK PRESS LLC
187 E Warm Springs Rd,
Suite B285 Las Vegas NV 89119 USA

Website: https://workbookpress.com/
Hotline: 1-888-818-4856
Email: admin@workbookpress.com

Ordering Information:

Quantity sales. Special discounts are available on quantity purchases by corporations, associations, and others. For details, contact the publisher at the address above.

Library of Congress Control Number:

ISBN-13:   978-1-965732-42-7   Paperback Version

REV. DATE: 04/30/2025

Miracle Of The Shattered Blade

ALICIA MORTON

Contents

DEDICATION

With great honor and respect, I dedicate this story to my lord and savior Jesus Christ who has inspired me to write about this experience.

I had been curious to know who God was since my early childhood. Like all children, I loved to laugh, run and play with family and friends, but still there were times I wondered about God and his supernatural power. It seems you could just look up to the sky and see the stars and heavens declare the glory of God.

ACKNOWLEDGEMENTS

I give special thanks to tee for her energy and help in typing my initial story;

Kirby and Rachel, for their encouragement to move forward; Jacqueline, for her wisdom in helping with good decisions; My siblings for their great ideas and imagination; My children and son in law Bennie for their inspiration and motivation; My pastor and First Lady, for their encouragement and prayers; and God, my Deliverer, for coming through in a time of need. Some of the words in this story are from court transcripts.

Also special thanks to the entire Workbook Press Publishing team for all their assistance.

WEDDING DAY STORM

On a dreary, rainy day in 1968, alicia and phillip were married in a little church. The rain was gentle at first, but as the hours passed, it came down in sheets. Alicia noticed how the sound of it grew louder as she waited for the ceremony to start. She almost wondered if it was a sign of some kind, but she pushed the idea out of her mind when she remembered that she was so happy to finally be married to Phillip.

"Momma isn't here yet," said Phillip's sister. "I think she may be stuck because of the rain."

"The wedding's starting soon. We could wait a few more minutes, but we may have to go on without her." Alicia didn't want Phillip's mother to miss their ceremony, but the bridal party was already in place and the music was about to begin.

The bridesmaids stood in place in their velvety green gowns looking anxious but ready. The music began and Alicia watched as they moved gracefully down the aisle, immediately forgetting about the buckets pouring outside. Her thoughts were on Phillip and their life together.

She anticipated becoming a mother and the excitement that comes with children, but first she needed to get down the aisle and exchange some vows. Phillip's mother finally arrived in time for the reception. "I am so sorry that I missed the ceremony! Oh, you don't know how sad I feel." Phillip's mother grasped Alicia's hands and a few tears rolled down her cheeks. "I should stay with you both tonight to make up for it." Phillip's sister looked at her mother with big eyes.

"Momma," she started, "I think they'd rather be alone on their wedding night, don't you? We can always see them after."

"Oh. Oh! Yes, yes, you're right." Alicia's new mother-in-law understood what she was about to impose upon and blushed.

The rain continued as the reception went on, but it didn't matter to anyone, especially not to Alicia and Phillip who were enjoying all the wedding reception activities.

Two years after getting married, Alicia was expecting her first child. She had already considered that her marriage to Phillip made them a family, but this new life they created together made it mean something more, as if it brought her closer to her spirituality. She was very careful the whole time. She ate well, took walks, and made sure to always take her vitamins. However, something didn't sit right with her. She was in her seventh month and there was stillness in her belly. She spoke with her coworker about it. "Jane, I feel as if my baby is much quieter these days. I don't feel him as much."

"Oh, they don't move all the time. Don't worry."

Alicia was not satisfied with this answer. There had to be a reason why there were no longer any flutters in her belly and it had been well over a day since she'd felt something. That night over dinner, she mentioned her concern to Phillip.

"Don't you think it's strange that the baby doesn't seem to be moving? Here, touch my belly." Phillip placed his hand over her stomach for a moment but could not offer any wisdom in the matters of gestation. He continued eating his dinner.

Alicia went to the living room after dinner with a heavy heart. Something had to be wrong, but she was too tired to continue such an exhaustive train of thought. She slept a while but was awoken by a painful pressure that scared her enough to make her call her doctor.

"Could be a false alarm," he said. "After all, you're only seven months along. Call again if it gets worse and we'll take a look at you."

She took the advice and tried to relax, but nothing improved. What started as pressure turned into a fever and she felt she might have the flu, or worse; the thought crossed her mind that the baby wanted out for a reason, and not a good one. When she started vomiting, she could no longer sit around at home waiting for the symptoms to pass. She called the doctor again.

"Something is wrong. I'm throwing up and the contractions won't stop." She could barely say each word over the phone without wiping some of the sweat off her forehead.

"Come to the hospital immediately. You could be delivering early."

Phillip rushed her to the hospital and when they arrived, some of the staff was already waiting for her. She was taken into an examination room where the nurse immediately checked for the baby's heartbeat. She slid the monitor over Alicia's belly and spread the goop all around it. Alicia could see the nurse's brow furrow a bit and she could tell something wasn't right. The nurse left the room for a moment and returned with another nurse. He too grabbed the monitor and slid it all around Alicia's belly and found nothing. It wasn't long before she realized that she would have to be very strong for the next few hours, and soon she was sedated and taken into the delivery room. Phillip waited anxiously in the lobby, wringing his hands over and over.

When she awoke the next morning, she moved her hands down to her belly and felt that it was much smaller. Soon enough, she was asking for her child wanting to know where he was. The nurse heard her cries and called the doctor to her room.

"I'm sorry, but your baby was stillborn. It looked like he may have been dead for three days because the skin all over his body was peeling."

"How can that be? I felt him move just the other day," she pleaded, her eyes already heavy with tears.

"I'm very sorry that this happened so far along in your pregnancy. Don't be discouraged. Talk to your doctor about trying again when you're ready."

Alicia was not one to give up easily. Though it took time for her and Phillip to accept this sorrowful disappointment, they tried again. Months went by and nothing happened, no matter how ready she felt. When her anxiety finally got so big, she begged to God to please bless her with a child. She prayed for this so hard and she felt it deeply in her soul how much she wanted to become a mother.

Indeed, her prayers were answered and she was pregnant again the next year. She took much more care this time around, even taking extra time off from work to ensure that she could be safe. All around she felt the blessings, especially from her colleagues who hosted a baby shower and luncheon to celebrate.

She was well into her fifth month when Harry, Phillip's half-brother, came to live with them. It wasn't a choice she made without some thought. Phillip had brought the matter up when he received a phone call from Harry's parole officer asking if his brother could live with him. "What do you think about my half-brother Harry coming to live with us for a while?"

"I've never heard of him. Why haven't you mentioned him before? What's he in prison for?" she asked as she caressed her belly.

"Well, he's had a lot of troubles since he was young. Mostly stealing things."

"But you hardly know him. How do you know it'll be okay to have him here?"

"I do know him some. I remember him as he was when he was little and I spent a lot of time with him. I don't know why he got into so much trouble when he grew up. Maybe he'll like it better living with a brother. He can't stand to live with his sisters. Maybe he's too loud for them and they just fight all the time. A male influence might get him sorted out."

Phillip didn't seem to take his brother's history too seriously, but Alicia had already made a reasonable assessment of what this man would bring into their home. Judging by the way his sisters rejected his requests to stay with them while on parole, she imagined that there was something very wrong with him beyond the desire to steal cars or whatever it was that got him into so much trouble. If so, much time in prison couldn't set him straight, what would?

Phillip brought over a picture of Harry and handed it to Alicia. "This is him," he said as she took it and stared at Harry's features. He left her alone with the photo and returned after a while to see if she'd made up her mind.

"I don't know. He may cause trouble." At these words, Phillip hugged her and she rested her head on one of his big, broad shoulders, barely reaching it.

"Phillip, when I saw Harry's picture, a strange feeling came over me. I can sense that he may be against me in some way."

"Oh, he won't be any trouble," replied Phillip. "You don't even know him."

"That's what I'm worried about," said Alicia.

Lord, she prayed, if you see fit for him to come and live in our home, then let it be. I just trust you'll protect us as a family including our unborn child.

FOOTSTEPS IN OUR HOMETOWN

In september of 1971, harry was released from prison on parole and moved in with alicia and Phillip. His first night, she tried her best to make him feel welcomed. They talked that night and he mostly shared about life in prison. The more they spoke, the more Alicia realized that he did not seem like the kind of man who'd been in prison despite that being all he talked about. He was so well-spoken and intelligent and she wondered how someone who seemed so smart couldn't keep himself out of jail. He'll do fine, she thought. Perhaps him living with them could make him a better person, she hoped.

The next day, Phillip left early for work and left them to have breakfast together. They ate at the kitchen table and talked some more, and Alicia felt they were becoming more acquainted with each other. She learned plenty about inmate relations and various ins and outs of daily prison life.

Eventually, she felt she had to ask him about his relationship with God. His immediate answer said it all:

"God has not done a thing for me, and as far as I'm concerned, Jesus can drop dead and I won't feel a thing."

The words stung Alicia's heart and silenced her for the rest of the conversation. She wondered, how can I help him?

She hoped that if they took him to church, he might change his mind about Jesus. A month after he settled in, they invited him to Friday night service where the pastor talked about the week being a time for special prayer to God for forgiveness and protection. He mentioned the wrath of God was upon the unfaithful and he saw danger ahead. They all prayed and Alicia felt restoration for the church and wondered if Harry was moved by this at all.

That night, several members of the congregation were involved in car accidents and other unfortunate mishaps which they all survived. Upon learning this, the pastor warned at the next service that it all could have been worse had they not prayed.

THE PREMONITION

licia was very thoughtful after that service and believed things really would have been worse had they not all prayed just before. She prepared herself for bed and found that she had some trouble sleeping, though Phillip was long gone into a world of shallow breathing and dreams. He seemed so far away, as if he'd left her alone in the room. She tried to join him by setting her head against the pillow and closing her eyes, but something seemed to enter the room just then. A strong presence startled her and she wanted to feel afraid, but she felt something much more profound and powerful.

Had God entered the room? It felt that way, and the more she explored the matter, the more she realized that she was in the presence of something massive yet without definite form. She opened her eyes and though she could not see exactly what was there, she felt its presence.

For a moment, she forgot to breathe and realized that she was also in less control of her own strength. She wanted to wake Phillip but then was compelled to face this on her own. Why would God come to me this way? She wondered.

The weight of his presence suddenly felt burdensome, as if it pushed her further down into the bed. She handed herself over to this moment, realizing that her strength was no match for His. Her surrender provided her with visions of other human beings in the world, all connected through God, as if he was holding them all in his hands. We're so blessed, she thought, so blessed to be in your hands.

Slowly, her strength returned and she lifted herself from the bed. She walked slowly through the house still wondering about this visit. She slipped into the bathroom to search her face for any changes, and she found that she was wearing a fearful expression. Why is my face so afraid? She wondered. Just then, another sensation came over her, one of death, and she realized that this was the message she was meant to receive. She felt something terrible was on its way, but she could not sort out exactly what it would be.

She made her way back to bed but had difficulty falling asleep as she sifted through the details of the experience. His realness is above human imagination, she thought, God is really real. At first, she'd been afraid, but she wanted to put this fear into the Lord's hands so that she could rest. When she woke up the next morning, the room did not feel as it had when God was there.

She'd always felt near to him in some way, but that evening was different, bringing her to a closer walk with God. Lord, I will never be the same she proclaimed, I have now seen the power of God as never before. To feel him in the room amplified her faith and made her certain of his greatness. She dedicated her unborn child to Him and prayed that he be healthy and protected from any danger.

A Strange Christmas Season

There Were Many Things That Needed To Get Done Around The House In Order To Prepare For Christmas. The baby was not ready to come yet, so Alicia still lugged him around in her belly as she hung decorations and did other work around the house. She thought about how she had felt at this same point in her last pregnancy when she'd lost the child, so she was rather mindful of her well-being. She had a conversation with God in her mind and felt she could hear him speak to her:

Do you remember when you were gravely ill with the flu and how I brought you back to health?

"Yes Lord, I remember."

One after another, she remembered various times in her life when she was very ill, as if he wanted her to think of those things just then. She eventually shrugged this thought away. She called her sister Tresha to let her know she'd be on her way to pick her up since they were going to buy a nativity set for the church Christmas program.

Alicia got into her car and when she tried to get the engine running, the starter seemed to be out. She went back into the house and got on the phone again to give her sister the bad news. They'd begun talking about other things when Harry interrupted saying he wanted to make a phone call. Alicia was only half paying attention to him. He interrupted again to ask, "Hey sis, can I borrow the house keys for a moment? I just need to get the wind off my head and get that door shut."

Alicia had not really paid much attention to his request when she handed the keys over. She had forgotten that the door had already been locked when she walked back into the house. The door didn't have a working knob, so the only way to keep it shut was by using the key on either side to lock it. She was still on the phone when he entered the room again, this time holding a long knife he'd fetched from the kitchen, the biggest one they owned. In his pocket were the keys Alicia needed if she wanted to run out the front door.

She froze when she realized what was about to happen, then hung up the phone without a word. Lord, I can't fight, you know I can't, she thought. Lord, this is your fight, not mine. Harry came closer and as she looked him in the eyes, she only saw evil. She nearly fainted at the thought of not being able to defend her child, and for a moment it seemed that doing so would be more relieving than having to be awake for what was about to happen. As he held the knife high above her he commanded, "Don't yell or scream. Lie down."

The phone rang and Alicia remembered hanging up on her sister just a moment before. "Answer the phone," he ordered again, "Tell whoever it is that you have something else to do and don't make it sound funny or I'll send this knife right through your heart." He watched her with piercing eyes as she picked up the phone to speak to her sister for what she feared would be the last time.

When she hung up, she looked up at him in disbelief. "Take off your under garment, lie down," he said just before forcing himself on her. The words that poured out of his mouth were alkaline and Alicia couldn't escape far away enough in her mind to not hear them:

You better please me or I am going to kill you. I'm not happy, I'm going to kill you.

With these words, Alicia somehow found enough strength to push him so hard that he flew several feet away from her. It was as if a strong wind had helped her push Harry far away from her. She rolled off the bed and trapped herself in a narrow spot between it and the wall. She felt how weary she was when she tried to stand. Harry watched her with eyes so narrow and furious, an anger she'd never seen before in any man. He reached her too quickly and beat her on the head with all of his strength.

Alicia fell three times and was in a daze, her movement already limited by the size of the baby growing inside of her.

Things were going dark in her mind when a voice suddenly compelled her.

Wake up! Wake up! He's fighting you.

It was a voice she didn't recognize, but it was tiny and angelic. She shook herself in an effort to regain her senses, but the blows to her head were not the end. Harry grabbed the knife again and brought it down on her as she lay on the floor. She tried to kick him away with what strength she had left but he was so strong. Deliver me, Lord, she pleaded. Then the verse from Job 13:15 flooded her thoughts: Though he slays me, yet will I trust in him. The words echoed over and over as she tried to crawl away from between the bed and the wall. As soon as she got on her feet, she ran out of the bedroom and into the living room. She almost didn't realize how heavily she was bleeding and the sight of it didn't seem to alarm Harry. He told her to shut up, as if she was some hysterical woman screaming irrationally.

When he got close to her again, her instincts told her to protect the baby at all costs. He motioned to stab her again and she grabbed the knife with her bare hands, feeling the blade against the plump skin of her palms. He shook the handle violently trying to shake her off of it. She used every muscle in her body to try to break the knife and render it useless, but the blade only bent slightly as it sank into her skin. The pain became too severe to hold on and she let the knife go.

BEHOLD HIS MIGHTY HAND

How Long Had This Been Going On And When Would It End? After Letting The Knife Go, She Felt More insecure. Upon reaching the peak of her distress like David from the bible, she called upon the name of the Lord in a loud voice. "Jesus! Jesus!" she yelled, as she felt her voice soar all the way to heaven, and reaching the ears of God. Behold, the Lord's hand is not shortened that it cannot save, neither his ear heavy that it cannot hear. (Isaiah 59:1, KJV)

"That's not going to do you any good," said Harry. Her heart trembled as she staggered with fatigue. Now her right leg was bleeding too and there was an open wound above her eye where he had beaten her. She collapsed face down like a rag doll and realized her weight was on her baby.

Harry walked away for a moment and she prayed again.

Lord, this man is evil and you are the only one who can stop him, but I don't know how you will do it. I know you are a God of power and miracles, and I need one right now.

She wasn't sure if she was dying or going into shock, but just then her body became stiff and numb. She could hear Harry's footsteps coming back to her again. He stood over her then kneeled and brought the knife down again, this time in her back. As if by a miracle, the knife could no longer hurt her. It broke into several pieces right down to the handle and Harry ran back to the kitchen for another one.

By the time he returned, he was facing Phillip who had just gotten home from work. Phillip saw the weapon in his brother's hand. "What are you doing with that knife?" he asked. He had not seen Alicia on the living room floor nearby. Harry pushed past his brother and ran out the front door that

Phillip had left open. Alicia slowly rose to her feet and Phillip turned to notice her. His face went pale. "Lord have mercy," he uttered with a strain as he realized what had happened to his wife. Suddenly, a sense of panic overtook her and she screamed, running outside to escape the sense of oppression that Harry left behind in the house. When her neighbors saw the state, she was in, they immediately called for an ambulance and the police.

Phillip came running after Alicia to examine the state she was in and a sense of guilt made him choke up.The police regarded her with much empathy as they listened to her explain what Harry had done. "He's out on parole," she shared, and one of the police replied, "We're going to find him and put him back in prison." The paramedics immediately checked her to ensure the baby was okay and she was soon taken to the hospital. She had not yet seen the knife for herself, so when Phillip and her pastor explained what had happened, she knew right away that it was God's mighty hand that saved her life and broke that knife into pieces.

It wasn't long before Harry's ego got the best of him. He called their pastor and asked, "Is she dead yet? Tell me so I can rest." The pastor did not dignify the question with a response. He then called Phillip.

"The police are looking for you," Phillip said.

Harry asked, "What am I wanted for, first degree murder?"

No one he spoke to would confirm whether he had killed Alicia after all, as if her death would sate his ego. More than a week after he attacked her, he had the brilliant idea to steal a car. Harry was casually walking past the local police station when he noticed several unmarked cars in the lot. He tried the handles on each car door until he found an unlocked vehicle with the keys in the ignition. He drove away in a hurry but it wasn't more than an hour before the Highway Patrol spotted him driving recklessly.

It was as if he wanted to be thrown back into prison, because when the officer asked for his license, Harry immediately confessed to stealing the car. "I needed to get away," he said. "I was planning on driving back home to Arkansas because I had got into a fight with my sister-in-law. She kept pushing me, so I cut her and hit her and knocked her down to the floor."

Harry felt disgusted after his remarks. The police arrested him and took him back to the police station where he had stolen the car. He was later questioned for further evaluation.

A Place Of Comfort

When alicia was released from the hospital, she didn't want to go back to the house where she'd been so brutally attacked. She moved in with her sister Lynette and her niece Marshawn. Her sister's home was a refuge for her, a place where she felt safe and comfortable. Lynette was a hospital worker so she knew how to care for people, and Alicia very much needed it after what happened with Harry. Lynette gave her everything she needed and Marshawn was a sweet source of hugs and cuddles.

Sergeant Splitz and Alice Handy, two police detectives, visited Alicia in Lynette's home and asked to hear her story. As she recounted the details, they couldn't understand how Harry, with such a sordid history, could have been released on parole. They had reviewed his criminal record and felt his release was a very irresponsible move. They shared his record with her and the size of his file was as big as a city phone book. Before ending their visit, they handed her a subpoena for an upcoming hearing.

By January of 1972, Alicia had to testify against Harry. She was eight months pregnant as she took the witness stand, from where she could see him sitting with his head down on the table. She was asked several questions, each one more difficult to answer than the last, but she summoned the strength to tell her truth. Phillip testified last, sharing what he saw when he arrived home that day. Harry was convicted of assault with intent to commit murder and grand theft auto, but the sexual assault charges were dropped.

Alicia continued to live with Lynette and Marshawn after the baby was born, and she remained there for months until Phillip found them a new home. This was her miracle baby, the one who survived and who somehow remained safe during one of the most harrowing events of her life. God had protected them both but she felt much better having a new home to go to.

PRISON ATTACK AND BREAKOUT

Harry kept himself quite busy while in prison. He attacked an inmate by hitting him over the head with a chair as he lay in bed. He almost put the man's eye out and this caused him to get transferred to another prison.

Chris riley, a correctional officer at harry's new location, was in charge of a work crew that helped with grounds maintenance. This was a small group of prisoners allowed the privilege of being outside of the prison in order to work. Harry was one of the inmates in this crew and he did a good job of following instructions and not leading on to what was really on his mind. He leaned over to jacob, one of the inmates on his crew, and asked, "what do you think of us gettin' out of here?" They talked a while and put together a little plan to escape as soon as they were let outside of the prison for work. Riley was not expecting rebellion, so when he called the inmates back in, harry and jacob held tight to their shovels and when his back was turned, they attacked him.

He pleaded with them, "what do you want from me? Don't hurt me!" They hit him several times then tied his hands with a belt they'd made out of twine. Harry stuffed a gag in his mouth to keep him quiet. When riley stopped struggling, they ran away. Chris looked up in time to see jacob and harry scaling the fence and escaping the prison, though his eyes were being stung by blood. The third inmate in the cleanup crew sat by and watched the attack but did nothing. Several minutes passed before a staff member spotted chris's body on the ground. Blood was streaming from his face when a medical crew arrived to help.

As harry and jacob ran, they came to a highway where a woman was parked by the side of the road. They forced her out of the car, knocked her to the ground, and stole her vehicle. They headed to los angeles.

The morning, they escaped, alicia had woken from a dream that made her feel shaken up. It was as if she could sense that harry was no longer contained, so when she saw the story on the news that he had escaped, she realized the dream must have been warning to alert her. She informed her family of the breaking news but still called the prison to confirm if he was still there or not.

"I was assaulted by this person in 1971 and I just want to know if he escaped your prison." She needed further confirmation to alert her entire family. The person on the other end of the line was quiet at first, and then answered her with concern.

"That's him. If you happen to see him in the area, please call us right away."

Harry and Jacob were found in a L. A. County motel and were immediately arrested. His attack against Chris was so violent that he was placed in a mental institution for evaluation and treatment. Upon learning this, Phillip felt he should visit his brother and talk with him. Against her better judgment, Alicia and the baby accompanied him.

They sat across Harry at a small table in the visitors' room. Alicia let Phillip do all the talking. She held her son close to her and listened. Phillip wanted to know the specifics of his breakout.

"Who hit Officer Riley?"

"I did," answered Harry and chuckled. This sent a chill through Alicia. "That man couldn't do nothin'. He turned red."

How can anyone be so cold-blooded? thought Alicia.

A woman approached the table and smiled at everyone. "Phillip, I want you to meet someone who works here. Her name is Jo Ann." Harry brought over the mental health technician who was assigned to assist him during his psychological evaluation. She greeted them warmly. Alicia and Philip responded back to her by nodding their heads and saying hello.

"Harry is doing so well! He'll return to the prison soon. He's just been making so much progress and I'm so proud of him" she shared. Alicia was amazed to hear the good report and progress Harry had been making while in the institution. The technician appeared to be doing a good job. She came on as someone who was good at working with people in general because of her personality. She also seemed to have gained Harry's trust in communicating with her freely. The atmosphere was calm and peaceful and Harry appeared to be happy there.

Although harry seemed happy he soon escaped the institution. He managed to steal another car and drove as far away as he could. It was a while before the institution realized he was gone. As soon as the police were notified, the manhunt was extensive. They researched old police reports to get a sense for where he might want to go and got a hit on Arkansas from the time he stole the unmarked police car. They called Arkansas police right away.

Harry and Jo Ann arrived at his mother's house in Arkansas where he introduced her as his girlfriend.

"I met her while she was giving me treatment to get all better," he said with his arm wrapped around Jo Ann.

"Does this mean you're doing better now, Harry? It's so nice to meet you, Jo Ann, please sit down and get comfortable."

Harry's mother set out some drinks and said, "You know, Phillip and Alicia will be arriving soon for a visit. It'll be so nice to have ourselves a reunion."

Harry shifted uncomfortably in his seat and said, "Alright, how about I head out to the store and get us a few more things then. Jo Ann, you can wait here and get to know my momma. I'll be back soon."

SWAT FIGURES IT OUT

When phillip and alicia arrived, they had not expected to see jo ann. When alicia saw her, she immediately recognized her and a chill ran down her spine. She knew harry had been missing, but did his mother know? She played it safe in case Harry was in the house.

"Mind if I use the phone a moment?" asked Jo Ann.

"No, go right ahead. Use the one in the bedroom," said Phillip's mother.

Jo Ann was on the phone for a very long time. Her presence felt like Jonah on board a stormy ship that's about to tear up any moment. The family was gathered in the living room when the house suddenly exploded with activity. Police officers had them surrounded while members of the SWAT team jumped through windows holding guns. Jo Ann returned to the living room and said, "I figured this would happen." She looked startled and yet not all too surprised.

"What's going on here?" yelled Phillip's mother. "What's Harry done now?"

Without a word, the police took Jo Ann away and they apologized for entering as they had, especially because Harry was not there. They explained that when the institution learned he'd gone missing, they quickly figured out that he was likely to return to Arkansas based on previous attempts to escape in that direction. Information led them to learn about the relationship with Jo Ann and what knowledge she may have on how he escaped, which caused them to want to bring her in for questioning.

STRANGER IN THE WORK PLACE

In An Effort To Make Harry A Better Person, A Rehabilitation Program Placed Him As A custodian at a hospital. While he made his rounds, he noticed a woman who he thought was quite pretty.

"What's your name?" he asked her. "Janet. I haven't seen you here before."

"I know. I'm new. My name is Harry." He smiled and extended his hand to shake hers. She took it gently and looked him right in the eyes, feeling a little nervous yet intrigued by his appearance. He seemed young yet worn, as if the years were showing their toll around his eyes.

Without an invitation, he showed up at her apartment a few days after they first introduced themselves to each other.

"May I come in?"

"Alright." Janet had hesitated at first, but then pulled the door open all the way. "Would you like a coffee or something?" she asked.

"Sure, I'll take it back." He followed her into the kitchen.

"Listen," Harry started, "I kind of don't have anywhere to go and I was wondering if you'd let me stay with you. It would just be for a while and I promise not to be any trouble."

"I don't know. I hardly know you." Janet grasped her mug with both hands now as she looked at Harry, trying to sort out what he was really after.

"It's just been hard for me right now. I haven't really figured out where I want to live and it'd be nice to have someone to talk to when I come home. You seem like a really nice lady and a great friend. Whaddaya say?"

She sipped her coffee and rubbed her chin as she considered his request. After a few moments of awkward silence, she acquiesced.

"Okay, but you will have to pay half of the rent."

"Deal! Can I bring my stuff over tonight?" He almost looked like a kid who'd just been given an ice cream cone.

"Sure, I'll help you get settled in."

Janet made up a space for him on the couch and set out some extra blankets and a pillow. She cleared out some dresser drawers and made space for his toiletries in the bathroom.

Though he was helpful at first, keeping things clean and splitting the cost of their utilities, his true colors began to show. He argued with Janet over the most insignificant things around the apartment. He waited for her outside of her office at work and followed her almost everywhere else that she went. He threatened her and made her feel afraid to the point of exhaustion. She was afraid to ask him to move out, but she tried anyway. He refused.

One afternoon, Janet was preparing to head out with her friend Sandy. As she grabbed her bag and jacket, Harry asked, "Can you stay away from here for a night? I want to have some friends over."

"No, Harry. I don't want your friends coming over here and invading my apartment. It's not right to force me to leave and you know it." He suddenly took to her the way he had Alicia, beating Janet's head and swinging at her with a knife he'd been concealing. She shielded herself with the jacket, but he plunged the knife into her chest anyway.

"Please!" she begged. "Harry, please stop!" "Quiet down. You'll be dead in two minutes."

She heaved as she lay on the floor bleeding out. "Leave me alone then. Let me die alone."

"Very well," he replied and went into the bedroom, confident that when he came out, she'd be dead.

She listened as his footsteps disappeared into the room and quietly made her way out the front door. Sandy looked up and froze in disbelief as her friend walked up to the car covered in blood.

"Let's get out of here. Take me to a hospital." Janet quivered with every syllable. On the drive, she passed out and later woke to the beeping of a heart monitor as she lay on a clean hospital bed.

TRAGEDY SPIRALS IN THE NEIGHBORHOOD: THE INVESTIGATION

Mr. Sanborne's neighbors knew him well. They knew that he was a meticulous man whose yard was always very neat and green and he never let a newspaper sit out on his porch past eight in the morning. He was a well-known school teacher and couldn't help but experience some popularity with his colleagues after he'd raised the test scores of his lowest-achieving students.

When his newspapers began to pile up on the porch, his neighbors figured something wasn't right. Even when he was sick with the flu, Mr. Sanborne had always fetched his morning paper. They also saw that one of his windows remained open for days, and this was unlike him. Every night, he closed and locked all of his windows before going to bed. It's something he advised his neighbors to do as well. After much speculation and peeking through the windows, both of his neighbors decided it was time to call the police.

When officers arrived, the neighbors explained everything that was unusual about Mr. Sanborne's house, down to the pile of newspapers and flyers on the porch. "He is very clean," they explained, "He's never left his newspapers out like that. One of his windows is open and we haven't seen him in three days. You have to understand, this man takes very good care of his house even when he's under the weather. You've gotta get in there and see if he's okay. He hasn't come to the door when we've knocked."

When they found a screen missing from one of the windows, the police suspected a burglary gone wrong. They entered the house and carefully inspected each closet and room. When they reached one of the bedrooms, they noticed open boxes of bullets on the floor. They reached a second bedroom and found what looked like a figure hidden under quilts. They approached carefully in case the burglar was trying to hide in a pile of blankets. What they found instead was Mr. Sanborne's body with injuries so severe that the officers were repulsed.

It didn't take long for an investigation to help pull together important details, like when Mr. Sanborne was likely killed (the newspapers he hadn't picked up were a strong indication of the date) and what instrument was used to bludgeon him to death. But the really telling pieces of evidence were the fingerprints Harry forgot to wipe off the window screen when he removed it to break into the house.

Harry's record startled the investigators as much as Mr. Sanborne's broken skull had scared the officers who first found him. Somewhere out there was a man with a streak of violence so frightening that they wondered who would be so naive as to not keep him in.

THE ALMIGHTY WAS THERE AND HEARD HER PRAYERS

It was a particularly beautiful day and the sunrise church was just ending its final service for the afternoon. Helen liked to stay behind to pray after everyone else had gone home, and today seemed especially enjoyable for it. She liked the way the church was quieter after sermons and loved the way the sunlight filtered through the stained-glass windows, as if God was pouring into the room and warming her skin.

When Harry entered the church, he noticed only a few people all sitting apart from each other in different pews. He'd had no business there, but as he'd been walking down the street, the church caught his attention and he felt a perverse compulsion to enter it. He was like a coyote sneaking into a chicken coop, and he was hungry.

Helen was kneeling in her own pew when Harry first saw her.

"Hello ma'am. Can you tell me where the priest is? I haven't been to church in a long time."

Helen looked up and smiled, then pointed at the priest who was still at the front of the church.

"Thank you." Harry took a few steps as if to walk toward the priest, but immediately doubled back. Helen looked up again and saw a gun he held at waist level.

"Get up," he commanded in a soft voice that no one but Helen could hear. He pulled her by the arm and forced her into a bathroom at the back of the church.

He didn't hesitate to make his intentions clear. "Have you ever had sex with a man like me? Take off your pants."

His attack on her was quick and Helen was in such terror that she hoped this was it, that this was all he wanted. When he was done, she pulled her pants back on and choked back a sob that had been stuck in her throat the whole time. She was afraid it would be so loud that he would hurt her.

"You got any money?" he asked. She reached for her purse and he smacked it away.

"Pull your sweater over your head," he said. "Don't look at me."

Helen guessed that he didn't want her to see his face clearly enough to identify him, so she obeyed. He hit her with the gun several times, breaking open the skin on her head. Then suddenly, the gun fell to pieces just as the knife had when he had stabbed Alicia. First, the clip fell, then the rest of the gun disassembled and bounced off of Helen's crouched body. Harry ran out of the bathroom and got as far away from the church as he could while Helen blacked out, her body slumped against the wall.

When she came to, she'd almost forgotten where she was. She stumbled as she realized what she'd just survived and walked back toward the pews where she found a woman who had still been praying. She had a terrible pain in her head and was still too dazed to realize how much she'd been bleeding. "Please help me." The words were barely audible as she interrupted the woman deep in prayer. The woman gasped when she looked at Helen's swollen face and guided her down carefully onto the bench. "Try not to move, dear. I'm going to get help."

"Please don't leave me," begged Helen. "I'm afraid."

"Alright, come with me now." The woman helped Helen to her feet and walked her to the church's office where there would be a phone for them to call the police and an ambulance. The woman sat her down on a chair while she made the call.

but Helen could no longer sit up. She blacked out and slipped to the floor.

Harry's forensic wisdom was such that he did not wipe his prints from the gun he'd left behind. It didn't take long for the investigators to realize he'd been the one to hurt Helen so badly.

DEFENSE ATTORNEY
SEARCHING

When the time came for harry to face trial again, alicia and phillip had already brought three more children into the world and were busy moving forward with their lives as best as they could. They did not expect to receive a visit from Cyndi Myers, an attorney who went to great lengths to find them at their new address. First, she searched DMV records. These took her to the house they'd lived in when Harry attacked Alicia. Cyndi asked neighbors if they knew where Phillip and Alicia had moved to, and they could only tell her that Phillip drove a tow truck and she'd likely find it parked outside their new home.

After driving around the nearby neighborhoods, she spotted a tow truck in a driveway and took a chance. She parked her car and walked up to their door where she was pleasantly surprised to be greeted by Phillip.

"Hi, my name is Cyndi Myers. I'm really sorry to be bothering you, it's just that I have some questions about your brother Harry. He'll be going to trial soon and we need some information."

"Absolutely, come on in." Phillip stepped aside and then escorted Cyndi to the kitchen table. Alicia had been busy with the kids and was a little reluctant to have another conversation about the terrible things that happened to her.

"This might be a good time to listen in to find out what kind of questions will be asked," said Phillip. Alicia considered this for a moment, then spoke with the defense attorney.

"This is just an informal interview," said Cyndi. "I'd like to record it to make sure I don't miss anything."

"Sure," agreed Phillip and Alicia.

"Phillip, can you tell me something about Harry's childhood and your relationship with him?"

"Yes," he began. "I am ten years older than him. As a young child, I talked with him a lot and we did fun things together, like he'd ride on my back and I'd carry him everywhere."

"At what age did he start getting into trouble?" she asked.

"Yes, at age nine he was stealing and it got so bad he later went into a juvenile detention center."

When the interview concluded, Cyndi thanked them for letting her into their home and said goodbye.

Court Proceeding
Now In Session

The prosecutor, timothy shultz, began with his opening statements. He spoke directly to the jury:

"In order to be eligible for the death penalty, there must be special circumstances. In this case, there was a burglary and a murder. There are two possible penalties: Life without parole, or the death penalty. You will be responsible for making the right decision on this man's life. Also keep in mind that this man's mental health is a huge factor in deciding just how responsible he is for the things he has done. Though insanity is not an excuse for the crime, it plays a factor in our understanding of why these things happened. Please examine all of these facts carefully before you come to a final decision."

Deputy Lois Mills presented the second half of the opening statement.

"This man has a rather extensive criminal history. He has felony convictions dating as far back as twenty years. On July 20, 1979, he attacked Helen Moore in a church.

She was brutally beaten and raped and left for dead. Just four days before that, he broke into the home of D. Sanborne where he stole a television set and then bludgeoned Mr. Sanborne to death. On December 4th, 1978, he attacked his roommate Janet by beating and stabbing her in the neck and chest. She was in intensive care and was hospitalized for six days. Four years before that, he attacked a correctional officer named Christopher Riley. Harry left Riley on the ground bleeding so that he could escape that prison. The reason he was in prison at that time was because he also brutally attacked Alicia, his sister-in-law. He beat and stabbed her while he was on parole. There is a very evident pattern of behavior, even down to how he chooses to attack his victims, which all have been hit in the head and/or stabbed."

Adam Shaw, the defense attorney, stood up and objected to that remark saying, "I would like to make a motion outside the presence of the jury."

The judge dismissed the jury until 1:30pm. He instructed them to not discuss the case or form an opinion until the case was submitted to them for a decision.

Shaw claimed he was constrained against his will and wanted to make a motion for mistrial. "The DA stated that all of Harry's victims were hit in the head and this makes Harry look guilty before any evidence has even been presented to the jury. The prosecution is creating jury bias against my client."

"Your honor, all we said was that all of the victims were struck in the head. We did not argue about what it meant, it was only a straightforward statement. I'm not sure I understand how this rises to the level of argument," said Shultz.

"How in the world was there any reason whatsoever to mention that all the victims were struck in the head? The only reason I can think of is that you are trying to influence the jury with respect to an unproven case."

"Anything further?" asked Judge Hagan. "No, your honor," replied Shaw.

"You are in recess until 1:15pm. I am not ruling a mistrial." Judge Hagan dismissed them to lunch.

The court's recess ended and the jury now had to listen to the defense's opening statements. Shaw began:

"Good afternoon, ladies and gentlemen. I'd like to talk to you about history, because history plays an important role in this case. There is one thing that overrides all other matters you will hear and that is the fact that Harry will probably die in prison. The only question for you, ladies and gentlemen, ultimately, is whether you will decide on his death, or if God will."

"Objection, your honor," said Lois Mills. "But that's the issue!" Shaw responded. The judge overruled it.

"Harry has suffered numerous convictions over the years. There will not be a lot of cross examination of witnesses. The attempted murder, rape, and robbery of Helen Moore is a case that has still not been proven to have been caused by Harry. Therefore, you must assume that he is innocent until proven guilty. The very next day after Ms. Moore was attacked, another woman named Sharon D. was raped by a man in a park less than two miles from the Sunrise Church. The police believed, to some degree, that the same person was responsible for both of these assaults. Sharon D. testified to being raped by a man and she would definitely tell you that Harry does not fit the description.

"I advise you to keep an open mind. Harry has paid his debts to society after his previous convictions. The prosecution will have you believe that Harry still has some debts to pay."

Mills objected. "This is argument." Judge Hagan sustained the objection.

"Judge, this is my sentencing authority. This is not like a case where I have a presumption of innocence," argued Shaw. "I am not in a position to be arguing to this jury, but it's the manner in which I will be presenting my testimony and evidence. I think I am entitled to quite a bit of leeway in an opening statement before the sentencing authority."

Mills stood up and said, "I'm going to object to counsel arguing with the court in front of the jury."

Judge Hagan remarked, "By and large, that is all right, but the objection is sustained regarding statements concerning the defendant's debts to society." Shaw took a deep breath and continued. "I did not mean to argue with the court. I should say that I do sometimes have a hard time making a point, so I take the long route. When Harry was convicted back in 1971, he went to prison for assaulting his sister-in-law. I mention this because some of you may feel he did not pay his debt to society. When he assaulted a fellow inmate, he did time for that as well." "Objection," demanded Mills.

"Sustained. I am dismissing the jury for fifteen minutes," said Judge Hagan, wanting to discuss these debts to society out of the jurors' presence. "Shaw, your statement appears to be implying that Harry has already paid his debts and that therefore he should not be sentenced to death."

"Oh, I see what the problem is. I'll clear it up before the jury. I guess I'm a little upset at the rudeness of the interruption. I heard a phrase this morning about the senseless killing of D. Sanborne. I'll qualify every statement that I tell this jury, but they were treated to a massive rendition of horror this morning, and I've got to deal with it." Shaw could think of no other way to help his client than to ensure that the jury did not hold prior crimes against him for which he had already served time.

The jury returned and Shaw continued with his statements on Harry. "Harry was born with head trauma which went undetected for years.

This could have had a direct impact on his mental health as an adult. Please keep an open mind as you review the evidence presented to you in this case."

The first witness to testify was a friend of Mr. Sanborne's. She knew him very intimately and shared that she was familiar with his lifestyle and what objects he owned in his home. She identified the stolen television set as having belonged to him.

The next witnesses to testify were the detectives who visited the crime scene in Mr. Sanborne's house. An expert from the Department of Justice testified that he identified and confirmed the latent prints taken from the Sanborne's window screen and the gun clip found at the church as belonging to Harry. The doctor who performed the autopsy on the murder victim testified to the extent of the severe blows he received. The surviving victims were the last to be called to testify.

Helen Moore testified of the rape and pistol-whipping she suffered in the church.

The correctional officer, Chris Riley, testified to how he was tied, gagged, and beaten in the head.

Janet took the stand and told how she was beaten and stabbed in the neck and chest.

The prison inmate who was attacked with a chair was deceased; therefore, his previous testimony was read aloud in court.

Alicia was the last victim to testify. She was not allowed to talk about the rape, but she did tell of the vicious beating and multiple stab wounds she suffered.

After Shultz's witnesses testified, it was the defense's turn to present its witnesses and experts. The first witness was a former elementary school teacher who remembered Harry when he was in the third and fourth grade. She shared that he was a very smart student who always finished his work quickly and was well-behaved, the typically good qualities of most average students.

Next, a series of psychologists testified. They claimed Harry's behavior could have been the result of not getting enough attention from his parents when he was a child. They mentioned that Harry came from a large family in which he had eight siblings. His behavior later in life was likely a reaction to feeling deprived of things among so many brothers and sisters.

When Shultz examined these witnesses, they brought up that none of Harry's siblings demonstrated violent behavior, so it would be difficult to say that Harry's home life contributed to his affinity for crime.

An expert on brain matters took the stand. Shaw asked what effect head trauma could have on an individual. The expert claimed that it may cause pressure on the brain if left untreated. He went on to say that there were various stages to this condition: early, moderate, and severe. Because Harry's condition had gone untreated for so long, it could very well have caused brain trauma and affected his mental and emotional stability.

Shultz attempted to prove that brain pressure had nothing to do with Harry's violent behavior. "Harry attacks when he wants to attack," said Shultz. "Harry attacked a prison guard after he was taken out on prison grounds toward an isolated area. Harry was fully aware of the advantage he had on Chris Riley. Harry clearly had a plan that he couldn't have executed had he no control over his emotions and actions. Isn't that, right?"

The expert responded, "Well, it could be."

"Harry waited very patiently while Alicia spoke on the phone and made sure that her sister suspected nothing. Then, he begins to brutally assault her. Would you say that his actions indicate that he is in control?"

The expert replied, "Well, I guess you can say he had some control." "Not only is he in control, but it's also clear that he knows what he is doing

Shaw brought Phillip to the stand. Phillip talked about his half-brother's childhood and what he could remember about the way they were brought up. Harry was born when Phillip was ten. They played a lot when they were young and he cared for his little brother. He shared that Harry had always been a smart kid.

"I left my home town and moved to the west. That's where I met my wife, Alicia. While we lived in Santa Monica, I got a phone call that Harry was up for parole and needed a place to live since no one else in the family would take him in. Nobody wanted him. We gave him a chance. My sisters were afraid of him, saying he'd threatened them before. I thought we could help him. I had no idea he would attack my wife the way he did. I think prison made him mean and evil."

Then, it was Shultz's turn. "Now, you assume that prison made him mean?"

"Yes," Phillip answered.

"How did Harry and your wife get along?" "They got along fine."

"Did you observe how your wife treated him?" "Yes, with kindness from the first day he arrived."

Shultz continued. "Your family was afraid to accept him into their homes, but even though you and your wife took him in and treated him with kindness, he ended up hurting the one person who was the nicest to him."

Phillip felt the words getting stuck in his throat. "Yes," he answered.

After the cross-examination of witnesses, both sides were given two weeks to prepare their closing remarks.

THE VERDICT

After the attorney's presented their closing remarks, the jury spent two weeks trying to reach a decision. Finally, court resumed and Judge Hagan asked, "Have you reached a verdict?" "No, your honor, we have not."

"Did you try to reach a verdict?"

"Yes, we tried, but we were unable to do so."

The prosecution was disappointed. The defense was jubilant over the mistrial as they had just saved Harry from a death sentence. Shultz's next mission was to decide whether to retry Harry or give up and allow the judge to sentence Harry to life in prison without parole. All they needed to do was gather new and relevant evidence to make Harry stand trial once again.

Several months later, Harry got himself a new attorney, Jonathan Chambers. Shultz remained as head prosecutor and a new judge took the case.

A New Session Begins

To prepare for the new trial, shultz renewed all charges against harry and added a new charge for the sexual assault of alicia. The defense tried to make a motion for the judge to disallow Alicia's testimony, arguing that it would influence the jury to believe that Harry was also responsible for Helen's assault.

"The charges made by Alicia in 1971 were dropped because of a plea bargain. When those charges went to trial, there was only a preliminary hearing. The final result was to convict Harry of attempted murder and the rape charges were dropped. Your honor, these acts should stand trial." Shultz wanted very badly to see Harry be brought to justice.

Judge Neptune said, "I realize the prosecution's stance on how the discussion of rape reveals motive for the crime. I also see that both victims, suffered severe ordeals.

However, it is my duty to abide by the law and make sure the jury is not influenced by another accusation of rape in this trial. To assure the defendant's rights are not violated, I am forced to rule in favor of the defense. Therefore, you may only examine one witness on her case of sexual assault."

"All right," said Shultz wearily. "They are both so vicious, but Helen's assault and rape is the case that we'll hear."

Just as in the first trial, the same witnesses were called to testify and be cross-examined. Shultz just needed to prove Helen's case, so they looked at her testimony very carefully. The defense threw out the idea of bringing Phillip in as a witness again as they did not want to give the prosecution the opportunity to question him on certain items.

The one thing Shultz did not want to see happen was for Harry to be given anything resembling a second chance. If the jury became deadlocked as it had in the previous trial, Harry would end up serving life in prison without parole

FINAL DECISION

The defense was anxious to know the jury's decision. They knew they needed only one juror to vote for life without parole to keep harry away from a death penalty and they knew the prosecution would probably not seek another trial if that happened.

Finally, on September 5th, 1992, the jury announced that they'd finished deliberating. Judge Neptune asked the jury foreman for their verdict.

"Yes, your honor. We the members of the jury find the defendant guilty as charged, and that the penalty recommended should be death in accordance with state law."

Judge Neptune agreed with the jury's' recommendation and Harry's was sentence.

While some of Harry's victims were able to move on with their lives, others could not, such as Mr. Sanborne who was sorely missed by his family, friends and students. The inmate whose eye he severely damaged eventually healed and was granted parole. He returned to a normal life as best as he could. Officer Chris Riley felt a sense of relief after the trial. He was glad to return to work after healing from his injuries.

Janet struggled for a long time to return to life as it was before Harry came along. Testifying against him in court was not easy and neither was healing from her injuries. Still, she worked hard to get back to a sense of peace despite the trauma of the attack.

Helen found strength in her faith and she was like the tree planted by the rivers of water; her leaf did not whither.

Phillip cared much for his brother but left with a clear conscience because he did everything, he could to get his brother on a better path of hope. "He's a smart man with a high level of natural intelligence," said Phillip, "but violence crushes that ability."

What Alicia needed most, besides her children and husband, was to keep busy. She found fulfillment in her work at the community college and this carried her forward and along with her faith, it made her stronger. She did not have time to dwell on bitterness because forgiveness heals the heart. she saw first-hand how the power of God can work in one's life.

No man is an island, deep within us is a longing to have someone special in our lives. We all need a source we can look up to in good times and bad times. We need to trust Him.

Alicia remembered someone she was taught about in her childhood whom she learned to trust as a way of life. Now today she understands what David meant when he said, "I had fainted, unless I had believed to see the goodness of the Lord in the Land of the living." (Psalms 27:13, KJV)

His goodness is forever.

As of the publication of this story, Harry remains in prison. With all the time on his hands, he continues to be an avid reader, learning as much as he can about various subjects.

Appeals for a change in his status may be still pending. The exact contents of those appeals are unknown.

ARTWORKS MADE BY THE AUTHOR

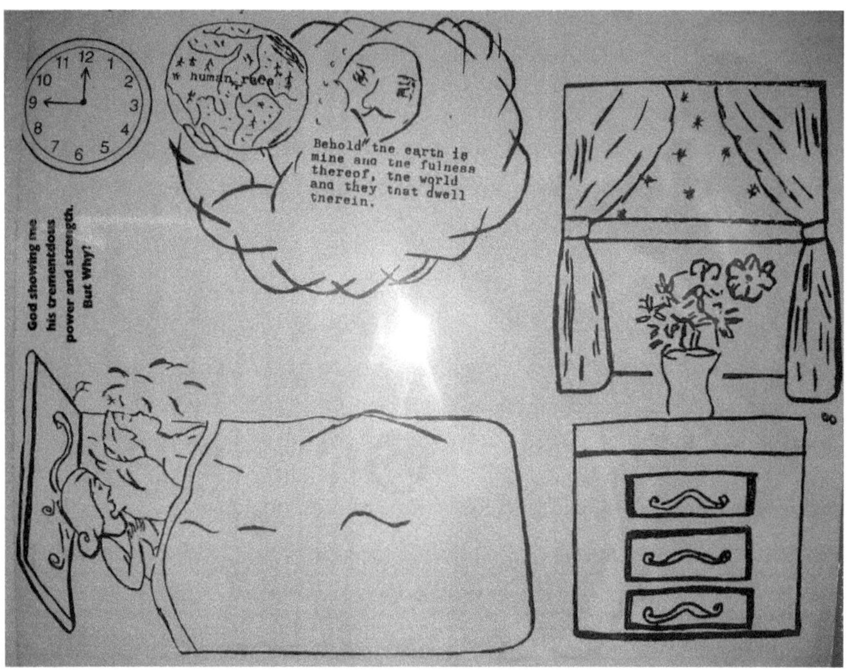

society.

Alicia
Phillip
Betty
Inmate William
Myra
Margaret
Inmate Jose
news reporter
Judge Frank
Defense Attorney Leonard
Judge Hagan
Janet
Helen
Attorney Adam
inmate
Christopher
Prosecuting Attorney Timothy
Sue
David

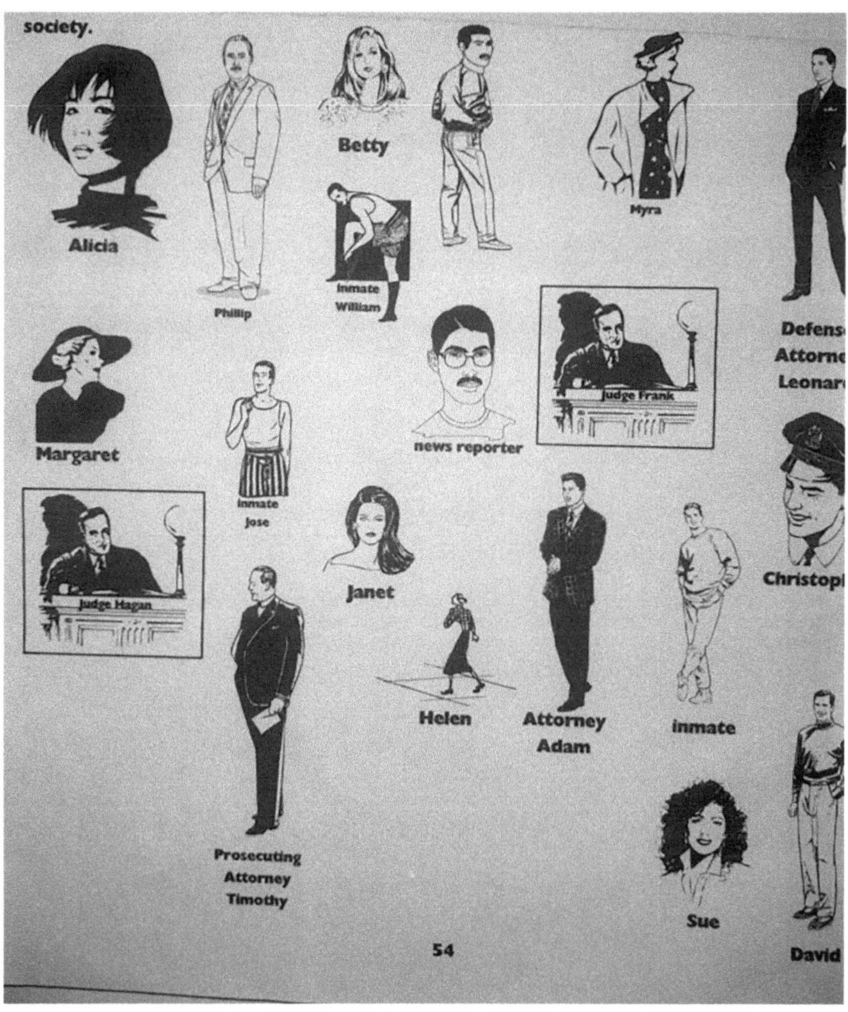

54

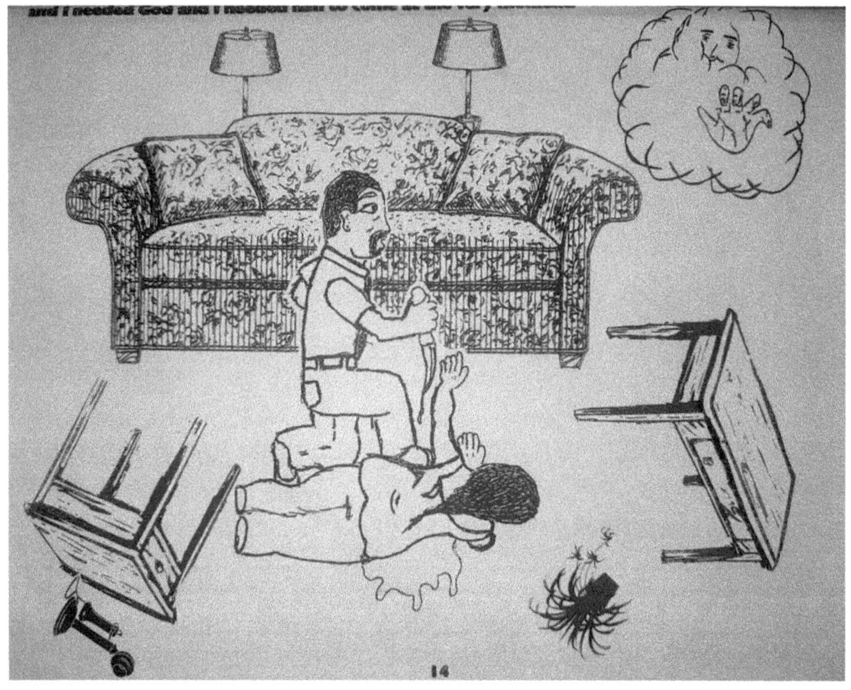
and I needed God and I needed him to come at the very moment
14

Open For
Prayer

Open For
Prayer